The fourth novel in J. I. M. Stewart's
brilliant Oxford sequence

There could be no question of the gravity of the
surveyor's report when it was given to the Governing Body a few days later. The document was alarm-
ing. The Governing Body, although an assembly
the awesomeness of which was such that I hadn't
yet ventured to open my mouth at it, was itself
awed by the dimensions of the crisis revealed.

Never having had to give thought to the prior-
ities enforcing themselves upon administrative as-
semblies, I hadn't thought of the overriding neces-
sity we were under simply to ensure that we had a
roof over our heads. It was the first rumblings from
the college tower that brought this home to me.

'Professor Sanctuary,' the Provost said evenly,
'favours the immediate launching of an appeal.' . . . .